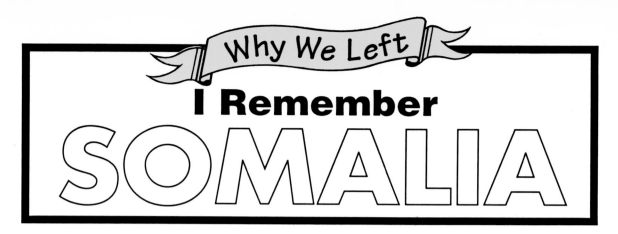

Why We Left

I Remember

SOMALIA

Jo Matthews

RAINTREE
STECK-VAUGHN
PUBLISHERS
The Steck-Vaughn Company

RSVP

Austin, Texas

Published by Raintree Steck-Vaughn Publishers, an imprint of Steck-Vaughn Company

Editors: Sally Matthews, Edith Vann
Designers: Tessa Barwick, Rob Hillier
Cover Design: Joyce Spicer
Illustrator: David Burroughs
Consultant: Ali Hassan Ali

Library of Congress Cataloging-in-Publication Data

Matthews, Jo.
    I remember Somalia / Jo Matthews; photographs by Tim Page.
        p.   cm. — (Why we left)
    Includes index.
    ISBN 0-8114-5606-4
    1. Somalia — Description and travel
— Juvenile literature. [1. Somalia.]
I. Title. II. Series.
DT401.8.M38   1995
967.73—dc20   94-25547
                  CIP AC

Printed and bound in Belgium

1 2 3 4 5 6 7 8 9 0 PR 99 98 97 96 95 94

Contents

Introduction

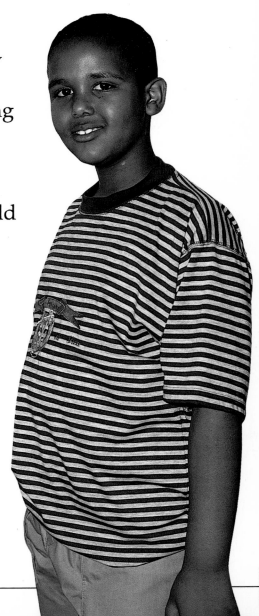

Hello! My name is Ali Hussein Jama, but you can call me Ali. I am 10 years old, and I come from Somalia. My family and I now live in the West. We had to leave Somalia because of many problems. They are tearing the country apart.

Almost everything here is different from Somalia. But I am getting used to my new home. You can help me to remember my old one by learning about it. So come with me now and discover Somalia. I'll tell you about its history, geography, and culture. I'll also tell about the traditions and way of life of the Somali people.

Over a million Somalis have fled to other countries. They left because of poverty, drought, famine, and civil war. Some refugees have gone to other African countries, and some, like me, have come to live in the West.

Welcome to Somalia

Somalia is a large country. It is located at the tip of the Horn of Africa on the east of the continent. There are about seven million people, slightly less than a big Western city like New York. But Somalia is only slightly smaller than the state of Texas. Nearly 65 percent of the people are nomads or farmers, living in the country. The other 35 percent live and work in the cities. Livestock, like sheep, goats, camels, and cattle, are important to Somalia. Most Somalis are very poor.

Ku Soodhowow

Soomaaliya

We speak Somali, which started as a spoken language only. In 1972, we gave it an alphabet. Now we can write things down. This means "Welcome to Somalia."

5

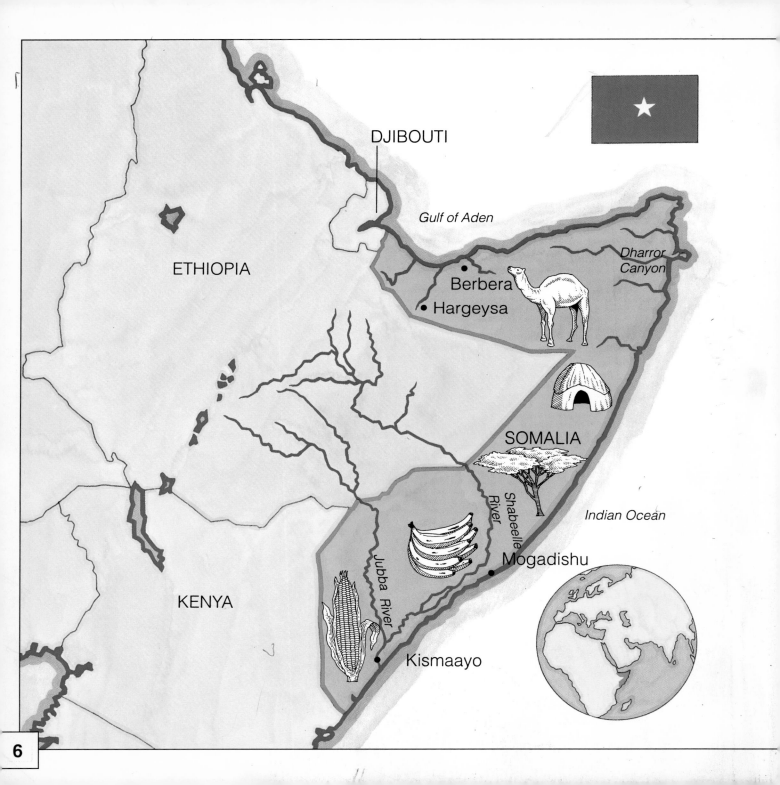

DJIBOUTI

Gulf of Aden

ETHIOPIA

Berbera

Hargeysa

*Dharror
Canyon*

SOMALIA

Shabeelle River

Indian Ocean

Jubba River

Mogadishu

KENYA

Kismaayo

Land and Climate

Somalia is on the east coast of Africa and is shaped like a seven. Its neighbors are Ethiopia, Kenya, and Djibouti. It has two coasts, the Gulf of Aden on the north, and the Indian Ocean on the south.

Most of the land is dry and dusty plains, with a few areas of grassland and a few acacia trees. Somalia is very hot, with temperatures between 86 and 104 degrees Fahrenheit (30 and 40 degrees Celsius). We have very little rain, sometimes none.

In the north there are mountains. In the south there are two big rivers, the Jubba and the Shabeelle. Most of Somalia's good farming land is in the area between these two rivers.

Water is Somalia's scarcest resource. People have to travel many miles to find water for their animals. Acacia trees are a common sight. Because they do not need much water, they can survive in Somalia's harsh environment.

The Ancient Land

Who the earliest Somalis were, and where they came from, is a bit of a mystery. It is believed that they first lived in the northeastern part of the country. Around the seventh to ninth centuries, they began to move south. At the same time, Arabs and Persians traveled to Somalia and settled on the coast. There they built cities. The Arabs introduced Islam, and by the thirteenth century, most Somalis had become Muslims. In the nineteenth century, France, Britain, and Italy divided Somalia among them. Somalia didn't gain its independence and unite as one country until 1960.

The buildings of Mogadishu (left) reflect the Arab and European influences in Somalia.

The ancient land of Somalia was called "Cape Aromatica" by the Romans because of its incense trees. Incense (right) is still exported today.

The People of Somalia

Most Somali people belong to a clan. There are two main clans. The people of the Samaale clan are mainly nomads. The people of the Sab clan are farmers.

A clan is like a big family or tribe. All members of our family, even the most distant ones, are part of our clan. Because the clans are now so big, we no longer all live together. But many of us still live in groups of families. Most nomads, for example, travel in groups of about ten families. The families of the original Arabs and more recent Arab settlers live mainly in the cities.

Family life in Somalia is very different from that in many western countries. Men often have more than one wife. Women keep their own names when they get married.

The women in the family teach us the history of our clans and country (right). This is called the oral history, *abtrisirno*, because it is not written down.

11

Life on the Move

Somalia is often called "a nation of nomads." Nomads do not live in one place, but travel across the plains. They stay in each place for only a few weeks before moving on. They do this to find new places for their sheep, goats, and camels to eat and drink.

Being a nomad means that everything you own must be easy to pack up and carry on a camel. Even your house must be movable! Camels are used because of their strength. They can cover hundreds of miles across the dry plains. Camels need water only about once every 20 days.

There are nomads all over the world. Some, like us, travel on camels. We also use camels to transport goods across the plains (far right). Other nomads, like the Romany Gypsies in Europe, use caravans or trailers. This traditional Romany caravan (right) is pulled by a horse. But today most are towed by cars or trucks.

We spend most of our lives outside, traveling, working around our camps, and caring for our animals (right). The only time we are indoors is at night, when we are sleeping. In developed countries, most people work in towns and cities. This means that they spend more time indoors, at school, in factories, and in offices (above).

A Nomad's Day

Instead of going to school, nomad children go to work very early. The boys care for the camels. This is a big responsibility, as they are very valuable. They must be fed and milked three times a day. The girls look after the sheep and goats, herding and milking them, too.

We spend much of our time traveling to new pastures. Children travel on the camels until they are old enough to walk with the adults. Sometimes we have to go into the cities to sell our livestock. We buy things we cannot provide for ourselves, like rice and sugar.

Our main diet is made up of milk and mutton, meat from sheep. We also eat rice with ghee, which is the oil from butter.

Nomads sleep in *aqals*. These are small, foldable huts made of wooden frames with animal skins or grass mats on top (right). They are a little like tents or tepees. They have to be easy to put up and take down each time we move. They must be light enough to carry on the camels. They protect us from cold nights.

Farming and food preparation are done by
ancient methods in Somalia, using human
and animal power. In developed countries,
machinery is used to do many farming
jobs. This girl is grinding grain to make
flour (left).

Farming

Somali farmers live in the fertile south between the two rivers. It is here that most of the main foods of Somalia are grown. The farmers grow a variety of crops like corn, millet, rice, sugarcane, citrus fruit, sorghum, and beans. There are also banana plantations, begun by Italian settlers along the rivers. Bananas are now one of Somalia's main exports.

The way of life of the farmers is very different from that of the nomads. Instead of moving around, they live in villages. Their houses are round, thatched mud huts called *mundols* (left).

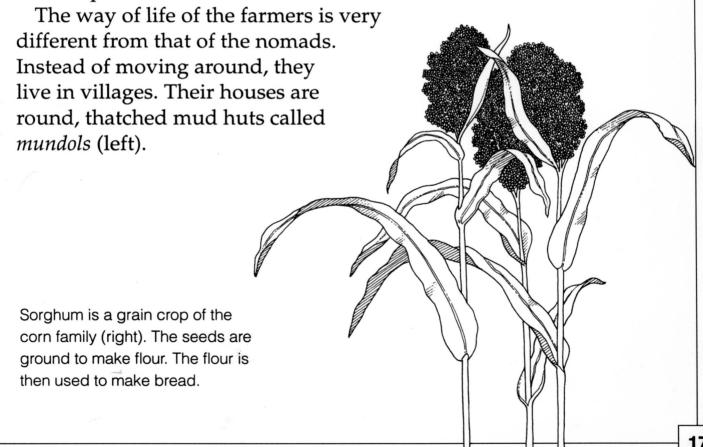

Sorghum is a grain crop of the corn family (right). The seeds are ground to make flour. The flour is then used to make bread.

Living in the Cities

Mogadishu, in the south, is the capital of Somalia. Other major cities include Kismaayo, Hargeysa, and Berbera.

The cities in Somalia are very different from Western ones. There are few roads, no railroads or buses, and no cars. In fact, only one percent of Somalis own a car. Most people walk everywhere. Some ride animals, such as camels or donkeys, and others get rides on trucks.

People come to the cities to buy and sell goods in the livestock and food markets. Craftspeople also make goods. They sell brightly colored cloth and beautiful leather work, like saddles and sheaths for daggers.

Many of Somalia's chief exports are animal hides, livestock, and bananas. They leave the country from the major ports of Mogadishu and Kismaayo (right).

Drought, famine, and war have made it impossible for most country people to maintain their way of life. That is why many have set up camp outside the cities (above).

This man is making clothes from Somalia's famous banaderi cotton (left).

Many Somali women wear a kind of dress called a *guntimo* (below). This looks like an Indian sari. Married women usually tie their hair back and cover their heads with a shawl called a *garbasaar*. Unlike many Muslims in other countries, Somali women do not wear veils.

Food and Clothes

We do not have to wear many clothes because it is so hot. But because of our religion, we cover our bodies properly. Most Somali people wear traditional clothes made from cotton. Some men wear white cloth hung over their shoulders. They wind it around their waist, like a Roman toga. Others wear colorful wrap-around skirts, called *masawis*. The traditional women's clothing is shown on the left. In the cities, some people now wear Western clothes.

In Somalia the main meal, *qado*, is at noon. We eat mainly milk, mutton, rice, and beans. Recently we have suffered terrible droughts. They have left many people without enough food to eat. This has caused people to starve in many parts of the country.

In Somalia, we have to prepare most of the food we eat. We cannot buy prepared food from stores, like people do in other countries (left).

The woman in the picture (far left) is preparing beans to make *digger and soor*. It is a mixture of boiled beans and corn, eaten by farmers.

Our Beliefs

Most Somali people are Muslims. This means that we follow the teachings of Muhammed. These are written in a book called the Koran. These beliefs affect the whole way of life, culture, and character of the people. For example, we do not drink alcohol or eat pork. One of our main religious events is Ramadan. It lasts for a month. Then we do not eat or drink in the daylight hours.

The Somali new year is at the beginning of August. In the rural areas it is celebrated by a big festival. This is called *Dab-Shid*, or fire-lighting. Every member of the household has to light a stick. Then they jump over the fire.

Somali people have many myths and legends. They believe it is lucky to see a Hoopoe bird (right). In one legend a Hoopoe bird warned King Solomon in ancient times. It told of the Queen of Sheba's visit to Somalia.

Somalis honor Muslim saints and make journeys to their tombs. One is shown above. There are also many places for Muslims to worship in Western countries. An example is this mosque in Manchester in the north of England (left).

Learning and Leisure

Few Somalis have televisions or radios. We have to entertain ourselves. Many people like to play sports, particularly soccer and basketball. Many children play hopscotch, too. We also have very few books to read. Most of our stories have to be remembered. We use poems and songs to tell them. We love to listen to a good song or poem after work.

Less than 20 percent of children go to school. The women teach the children at home. However, about 60 percent of Somalis cannot read or write. But we have developed a way to keep up with the news. Whenever we meet someone, we ask a set of questions. We ask about what is going on in our country. Then we ask about the rest of the world (left).

We love to play a good game of soccer. Many of us cannot buy soccer balls. We make our own out of paper and string. Or we use any other suitable materials we can find (right).

Somalia Today

Today Somalia suffers greatly from drought, famine, and war. Mohammed Siad Barre, the last Somali dictator, ruled the country for 22 years. When he was overthrown in 1991, the clans emerged. They were fighting for power. All of Somalia has become a battlefield — the cities, the plains, and the villages. The common Somalis can no longer farm or travel in their usual way. It is too dangerous. This has made it more difficult for them to survive. Hundreds of thousands have died. Over a million have fled to safety in other countries.

Large international efforts have been made to stop the fighting and restore order. Still, the conflict continues today.

Many countries have sent aid to Somalia. They have sent food and medicine (far left).

In 1992, the United States launched "Operation Restore Hope." They sent troops to make sure that the aid reached the people who needed it (left). The United Nations (symbol right) has now taken over from America. The UN will try to stop the fighting and help form a government.

Living in the West

It was not easy to settle in the West. It is so different from Somalia. At first, the clothes, the weather, the language, and the food seemed very strange. However, I am getting used to my new home now. I like going to school. I have many new friends who are of different races and religions.

I still miss Somalia. I miss the scorching heat, the animals, the ancient way of life. I also miss my old friends (right). I hope that the fighting stops soon. One day, I hope to be able to go back. I want to use what I have learned here to help rebuild my country.

"When elephants fight, the grass gets trampled." This is an old African saying that rings true for Somalia. If the elephants—the warlords—go on fighting, the people will be stepped on like the grass. I hope the elephants stop fighting soon and let the grass grow again.

Fact File

Land and People

Official Name: Jamhuriyadda Dimugradiga Somaliya (Somali Democratic Republic)

Languages: Somali, Arabic (both official)

Population: 7 million (approximately)

Population distribution: 65 percent rural, 35 percent urban

Cities

Capital city: Mogadishu

Other major cities: Kismaayo, Hargeysa, Berbera, and Marka

Weather

Climate: Hot and dry, frequent droughts

Temperature: 86–104 degrees Fahrenheit (30–40°C)

Annual rainfall: 11 inches (average)

Landmarks

Biggest rivers: Jubba, Shabeelle

Highest mountain: Mount Surud Ad, 7,900 feet above sea level

Government

Form of government: Socialist Republic

Head of state: President

Eligibility to vote: All citizens 18 years and over

Culture

Main religion: Sunni Islam

Literacy rate: 40 percent

Trade and Industry

Manufacturing: Sugar

Employment: Raising livestock is the main form of employment (60 percent). Others include farming, crafts, and trading.

Currency: Somali shilling

Food and Farming

Area: 246,200 square miles (637,657 sq km)

Land use: Cultivated 2,656,000 acres (1,075,000 ha)

Grazing area 71,289,000 acres (28,850,000 ha)

Forest and woodland 21,226,000 acres (8,590,000 ha)

Other 59,836,000 acres (24,215,000 ha)

Vegetation: Grass, acacia trees

Major crops: Rice, corn, millet, sugarcane, citrus fruit, bananas, sorghum, and beans

Livestock: Sheep, goats, camels, and cattle

Index

Photographic Credits:
Special thanks to Panos Pictures, who supplied all the pictures in this book except: Front cover inset, p. 3, p. 14 (left), p. 21, p. 28: Roger Vlitos; title page, p. 8, p. 16 (bottom): Hutchinson Library; p. 12: Spectrum; p. 23 (bottom): Paul Nightingale